This

Postman Pat

book belongs to:

. . . .

D1642899

More Postman Pat stories:

Postman Pat makes an aeroplane
Postman Pat takes a photo
Postman Pat mends a clock

First published 1999
by Hodder Children's Books
a division of Hodder Headline plc
338 Euston Road, London NW1 3BH

Story copyright © 1999 Ivor Wood and John Cunliffe
Text copyright © 1999 John Cunliffe
Illustrations copyright © 1999 Hodder Children's Books
and Woodland Animations Ltd

HB ISBN: 0 340 73714 X
PB ISBN: 0 340 73715 8
10 9 8 7 6 5 4 3 2 1

A catalogue record for this book is available
from the British Library.
The right of John Cunliffe to be identified as the
Author of this Work has been asserted by him.

Printed in Italy.

Postman Pat

and the sheep of many colours

John Cunliffe

Illustrated by Stuart Trotter

from the original television designs by **Ivor Wood**

Hodder
Children's
Books

a division of Hodder Headline plc

Winter was coming on.
It was dark by tea-time.
"I don't like these dark
nights," said Pat.
"You need a hobby,"
said Sara. "Something to do."
"That's a good idea," said Pat.
"You can start with window-
cleaning if you like,"
said Sara.
"I was thinking," said Pat,
"of something more like . . .
well . . . I'll have a think . . ."

The next day, Pat had a parcel for Miss Hubbard.
"Oh, hello, Pat!" said Miss Hubbard. "Good man,
you've got my parcel.
It must be my new colours!"

She snipped the parcel open. It was full of little pots of colour: lovely bright colours - red, blue, green, orange - dozens of them. She had covered the table with newspaper, and she had a big bowl of water on it.

"You look busy," said Pat. "Whatever are you doing?"
"Marbling," said Miss Hubbard.
"I used to play marbles when I was a boy," said Pat,
"but we never did it with pots of paint."

"Not marbles," said Miss Hubbard. "This is marbling. Look, you put these colours on top of the water. Then you stir it round a bit."
"What a lovely pattern," said Pat. "I wish I could do that."

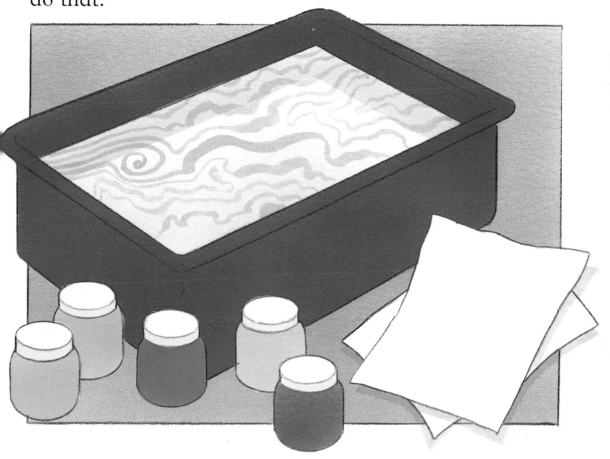

"It's quite easy," said Miss Hubbard.
"But watch what I do next."

She laid a piece of paper on the water,
then peeled it off again. The pattern
was on the paper, now.
"My goodness!" said Pat. "I do wish
I could do that. It's wonderful!"
"Tell you what," said Miss Hubbard,
"come for tea on Sunday, bring Sara
and Julian, and you can all have a try."

They had a lovely tea, with cheese sandwiches, and cream cakes. Then they cleared the table. Miss Hubbard gave everyone a big apron, and they set to work. Such patterns they made! The colours swirled and splashed, and melted and merged, and the patterns seemed endless.

They rigged up lines of string to hang the drying paper on, and the little house was soon full of them.

When they were dry, Miss Hubbard
put them in a box for Julian to take home.

Soon, everyone in Greendale wanted to have a try.
Pat had lots of parcels of paint to deliver.
The whole of Greendale went marbling-mad!
They covered all the hymn books in the church
with marbled paper.

The children covered
their books at school.

Granny Dryden made a
marble-cake, and covered
it with marbled icing.
(She used special colours
that were safe to eat.)

Mrs Goggins made some marbled
envelopes to sell in the post-office.
"They're lovely," said Pat,
"but I can't see the addresses!"

One day, Pat delivered a parcel of marbling-paints to
Dorothy Thompson, just as Alf was dipping the sheep.

No-one noticed that young Bill had opened the paints, to have a look at them. He had stood the little bottles all along the top of the fence by the sheep-dipping place. When Alf banged the gate, the fence shook and wobbled. Every one of those bottles went plop into the sheep-dip. When the sheep came out . . .

. . . they were all the colours of the rainbow.
What a sight they were!

The colours did the sheep no harm. People came from far and near to see the famous marbled sheep of Greendale.

That was the end of the Greendale marbling craze, but they still have the brightest hymn-books in the kingdom. The sheep were sheared long ago.
As Alf said,
"Our sheep are black and white and brown, now, just like any other sheep."

More Postman Pat adventures:

Postman Pat and the Mystery Tour
Postman Pat and the Beast of Greendale
Postman Pat and the robot
Postman Pat takes flight
Postman Pat and the big surprise
Postman Pat paints the ceiling
Postman Pat has too many parcels
Postman Pat and the suit of armour
Postman Pat and the hole in the road
Postman Pat has the best village
Postman Pat misses the show
Postman Pat follows a trail
Postman Pat in a muddle
Postman Pat: Four Square Meals